MAMA LION
WINS THE RACE

JON J MUTH

SCHOLASTIC PRESS • NEW YORK

Mama Lion and Tigey looked out their window into a beautiful morning.

"Today is race day!" said Tigey.

"Yes, it is!" said Mama Lion. "Are we ready?"

"Almost," said Tigey. "There are just one or two things we need to do."

"I will get our car!" said Mama Lion.

"And I will check our route," said Tigey.

"We're going from here — all the way to here!"

While Tigey tuned up their car, Mama Lion noticed Tigey's cup.
It was worn and dented, and had a hole in it.

"I wonder what the prize will be for the winner," said Mama Lion.

"I don't know," said Tigey.

"Maybe *we* will win," said Mama Lion.

"We *have* to win!" said Tigey.

"Well," said Mama Lion. "Winning is fun, but it isn't everything."

The town square was full of excitement.

"There are the Flying Pandinis in car number 3," said Tigey.

"And look!" said Mama Lion. "The Knitted Monkey crew has a banana on their car."

"And there is Bun Bun with her motorcycle," said Tigey.

Mama Lion and Tigey passed by the table with all the prizes.

First place was a big, fancy trophy.

Second place was a nifty small cup. *Hmmm*, thought Mama Lion.

Third place was the special Banana Issue of *Monkey Monthly*.

"Let's go," said Mama Lion. "It's time to put on our goggles."

Everyone watched as the Owl-fficials
called out:
"LADIES AND GENTLEMEN!
TAKE YOUR MARKS . . ."

"GET SET . . ."

The crowd grew silent.
The moment grew long.

The racers
charged forward!
The Knitted Monkeys
broke a rule and threw their smallest
crew member ahead.
Penalty whistles blew.
The monkeys grinned, then
they apologized.

Engines roared.

Spectators on the streets waved and cheered.

They were off!

First a sharp bend to the right —
then a second to the left!
The leaders moved swiftly out in front!

As they crossed the river,
Mama Lion and Tigey took
the lead . . .

. . . and soon they sped far ahead of the other cars!

Mama Lion noticed the warm wind and the fresh smell
of the grass as they breezed through the gentle hills.
The world is beautiful, thought Mama Lion.

They hurried farther along and passed two
children in their front yard with a puppy. They waved.
The world is friendly, thought Mama Lion.

Then Mama Lion caught sight of the Flying
Pandinis not far behind and thought, *The world is . . .*
Wow! The Flying Pandinis are zooming up FAST!

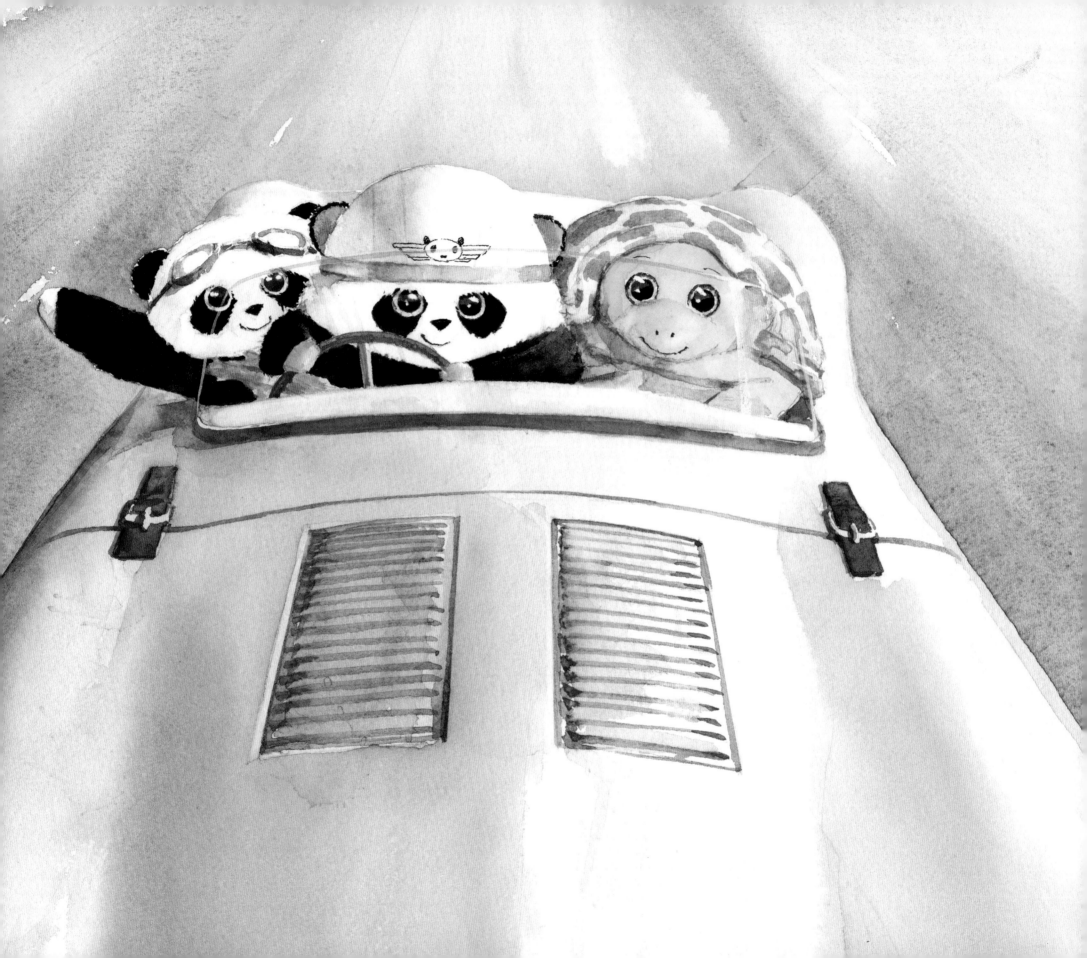

Suddenly, something appeared in the road ahead.

"Watch out!" said Mama Lion.

"Hold on!" said Tigey as he swerved and skidded to a stop.

"Oh, no!" said Tigey. "Our wheel has come off!"

"Yes, it has," said Mama Lion. "But you are a very skilled driver. This butterfly was not harmed."

"Pop the trunk and grab our tools!" said Tigey. "We must get on the road again!"

The roar of an engine drew close behind them. Gravel crunched and brakes screeched as the Flying Pandinis ground to a stop.

"Hurry, we must help them!" said Baby Panda.

"Yes! Look sharp!" said his sister Bao Bao. "They are using a number 8 spanner when they need a number 12!"

The Pandinis quickly bounced out and rolled over to the car. Mama Lion and Tigey stepped aside. The Pandinis were master mechanics and could fix anything.

Just then, Mama Lion saw Bun Bun pass by. She was scattering seeds from her bag.

"She will come back and water them after the race," said Tigey. "I've seen her do that before. Bun Bun is really good with plants."

"She is a very interesting bunny," said Mama Lion.

Suddenly, another car streaked past them.
"There go the monkeys!!!" said Tigey.
"We'd better go, too!" said Mama Lion.
They thanked the Pandinis, and everyone rushed back into their cars.

Mama Lion and Tigey sped off, their car running better than ever.

They were already gaining on the Knitted Monkeys.

To hold the lead, the Knitted Monkeys were up to their old tricks.

"Oh, no!" said Tigey. "We are getting close to the finish! I don't know if we can win."

"Just do your best, and keep on going, Tigey!"

Suddenly, the Flying Pandinis
came up from behind.
  Their car was stuck in reverse —
so they were driving backward!
  The monkeys, overcome by
ambition, dropped even more
banana peels!

The slippery peels sent the Pandinis into a skid. This
popped the gears and spun their car in the right direction.
In a dazzling performance, they picked up speed.

Mama Lion and Tigey raced ahead.

"Tigey," said Mama Lion, "here is our chance to do something *really* amazing!"

"Yes!" said Tigey. "We can win!"

"Or," said Mama Lion, "we could *not* win!"

Tigey blinked. He looked ahead to the finish line.

It was so close.

But Tigey understood.

Mama Lion reached over and pulled up the hand brake to slow them down.

The checkered flag fell and the Flying Pandinis zipped through the finish line in first place.

Mama Lion and Tigey came in a close second, and the Knitted Monkey crew placed third.

Back at home, Mama Lion poured some nice hot cocoa into Tigey's beautiful new cup.

"Those amazing Flying Pandinis stopped to help us, even though it meant they could lose," said Mama Lion. "There aren't many friends in this world who would give up winning a race for you. I would say that we won some very good friends today."

"Mama Lion," said Tigey. "I am very glad
we were in this race together."
"Me too," said Mama Lion.

For David Saylor!

With ineffable thanks to Dianne Hess,
Allen Spiegel, and my wife, Bonnie.

Thank you to The Light Brigade: Mo Willems,
Dave McKean, and Scott Morse.

To all the generous children and adults who
introduced me to their stuffed friends, thank you.

To the mutinous rapscallions Ava for Bun Bun;
Caroline for Kippy; Alex for Officer Teddy; Molly
for Tigey; and Leo for Mama Lion — thank you!

Copyright © 2017 by Jon J Muth

All rights reserved. Published by Scholastic Press, an imprint
of Scholastic Inc., *Publishers since 1920*. SCHOLASTIC, SCHOLASTIC
PRESS, and associated logos are trademarks and/or registered
trademarks of Scholastic Inc.

Library of Congress Cataloging-in-Publication Data
Names: Muth, Jon J, author, illustrator.
Title: Mama Lion wins the race / by Jon J Muth.
Description: First edition. | New York : Scholastic Press, 2017. |
Summary: Mama Lion, Tigey, the Flying Pandinis, and the Knitted
Monkeys compete in a road race, and when the Pandinis stop to
help Mama Lion, she is happy to return the favor.
Identifiers: LCCN 2015028630 | ISBN 9780545852821 (alk. paper)
Subjects: LCSH: Racing—Juvenile fiction. | Animals—Juvenile
fiction. | Helping behavior—Juvenile fiction. | CYAC: Automobile
racing—Fiction. Animals—Fiction. | Helpfulness—Fiction.
Classification: LCC PZ7.M97274 Mam 2017 | DDC [E]—dc23 LC
record available at https://lccn.loc.gov/2015028630

Detail on page 9 of Clifford from *Clifford, the Big Red Dog* by
Norman Bridwell. Copyright © 1969 by Norman Bridwell. Used by
permission of Scholastic Inc. Detail on page 9 of the Pigeon from
Don't Let the Pigeon Drive the Bus! by Mo Willems. Copyright
© 2003 by Mo Willems. Used by permission of Mo Willems and
Wernick & Pratt Agency, LLC.

10 9 8 7 6 5 4 3 2 1   17 18 19 20 21
Printed in China 38
First edition, August 2017

Book design by Charles Kreloff and David Saylor
Jon J Muth's artwork was created with Caran d'Ache pencils,
Italian writing ink, watercolors, and gouache on Moulin Du Roy
watercolor paper.